MW00936719

PIE CRUMBS & HIT AND RUN

CHRISTIAN COZY MYSTERY

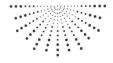

DONNA DOYLE

PUREREAD.COM

CONTENTS

AMERICAN AS APPLE PIE

Sammy hustled into the kitchen, a smile on her face as she felt the heat of the room envelop her. It was already hot enough outside, and the old air conditioner at Just Like Grandma's didn't do a good job of keeping up. But in the kitchen it was the type of heat created from making delicious food for the people of Sunny Cove, the heat from moving quickly and happily, and Sammy found that she enjoyed it. Johnny whistled to himself, bouncing on his heels as he listened to a baseball game on the radio, flipping burgers with gusto every time his team made a hit.

"I don't know how you can possibly follow along with what they're doing and still keep your orders straight," Sammy said with a smile as she pulled a chilled board out of the freezer and plopped a big blob of pie dough onto it. "Every time they start calling out statistics, I have to start measuring all over again."

Johnny grinned at her and swung his spatula like a baseball bat. He never said much, but he always managed to get his point across.

"You get used to it," said Kate, the latest hire at the restaurant. She had her dark hair pulled into a slick bun against the heat of the day, but beads of sweat stood out on her forehead as she scooped a serving of steamed broccoli onto a plate. "My dad listens to baseball on the radio all the time. He always used to tell me it was as American as apple pie, and we weren't patriots if we weren't cheering on our favorite team."

"How about strawberry rhubarb pie instead of apple?" Sammy asked. She kneaded the dough, relishing the cool feeling of it around her fingers. It was the perfect season for pies, especially with a big dollop of ice cream on top.

Kate tipped her head to one side, considering. "I don't think I've ever had it, to be honest."

"Then you're in for a treat. It was always one of my favorites as a kid. I like just regular rhubarb pie, too, but I thought the strawberry version might go over better." Sammy could clearly remember the first time she'd ever had rhubarb pie. Their neighbor was an old man that she never would've thought capable of baking something. But he'd invited them over after he had harvested a big batch of the long, green stems from his backyard and presented Sammy and her father with a rather sad-looking pie in a square dish. It was amazing, tart and sweet and cold and buttery. Sammy had instantly asked for more, bringing a big smile to the old man's face.

Sammy hoped to bring similar smiles to the faces of the customers at Just Like Grandma's. Her job was a lot of work, but it was so rewarding. She grabbed her favorite rolling pin, a heavy marble affair with beautiful swirls of gray and white. It made the work easy, and it could be chilled to keep the butter in the crust from melting even on the hottest of days.

Helen came bursting in from the dining room with a stack of clattering plates and cups, setting them down next to the sink with a thump and then wiping her brow. "I think they'll eat anything we give them right now, strawberries or not," she gasped. "I can't believe how busy we are!"

Kate peeked through the small window in the door to the dining room, her eyes widening in surprise. "I think you hired me under false pretenses, Helen. I thought I was coming to work at a cozy little café where the same old men came in every morning for a cup of coffee. But you've got a whole crowd of people around the entryway just waiting to be seated."

Johnny came and looked through the little window, quickly turning back to his grill so he didn't fall behind on orders.

"Don't I know it. But the Radical Grandmas are out there, talking their heads off and not moving an inch from that table no matter who might need it. Julia Richardson has brought in a handful of her cronies to work on some fundraising event for charity, even though we all know it's just an excuse for them to show off their wealth. Not to mention the rest of Sunny Cove!" She put her hands in the air as she grabbed a stack of clean plates and began plating up the buns for the burgers Johnny was working on.

"Nobody wants to heat up their kitchens and pay for the extra air conditioning," Sammy reasoned as she turned back to the fridge for the bowl of pie filling she'd prepared earlier, letting the strawberries and rhubarb chunks sit in a mixture of sugar, lemon juice, and cinnamon. "It's probably a lot easier to get out and buy something than to make it yourself when you're already thinking about how much the electric bill is going to be this month."

"I think they're just here for the pie, actually," Helen replied with a grin. "The bakery table is practically empty again. I've got half a pie under glass at the moment, but you know that's not going to last very long."

"I'm doing my best, I promise!" Sammy felt the pressure, but she didn't rush as she carefully laid her crust in a pie pan, trimmed the edges, and spooned the filling inside. She cut several chunks of real butter to go over the fruit, which really added to the flavor. The top crust would come next, and whether she did a lattice crust or a solid one with cute cutouts, she knew the appearance was just as important as the taste. The customers would wait, or they would come back for a slice the next day. They were loyal like that.

It was one of the many reasons Sammy was so glad she'd stayed on at Just Like Grandma's. She'd seriously considered opening her own bakery just a few months ago, something that seemed like a fantastic idea at the time. With her own place, Sammy could focus entirely on baking instead of ducking out of the kitchen every now and then to act as waitress or busser or cashier. Her efforts had been thwarted when the deal on the building she wanted to rent fell through, among other problems with the landlord. Although she was still keeping the idea in the back of her mind, she was content to stay at the restaurant for now. Those regulars out there who refused to leave their tables until they were good and ready, as well as those who were willing to stand in line just to get a seat at one of the battered tables, who anxiously watched Sammy walk out to the baked goods table in the corner to see what Sammy's special was that day, those were her kind of people. She would've missed them terribly.

"I know you are, dear. I can't think of what might've happened to this place if you hadn't come along. We were hardly doing any business at all, and for awhile I thought I might have to close the doors permanently." Helen smiled at her, her dark eyes twinkling fondly.

This knowledge surprised Sammy enough to look up from her work. "I don't think you ever told me that."

Helen waved it off with an arthritic hand. "It wasn't anything I was certain about yet, and I'm a firm believer in not scaring people unless there's a good solid reason. But everyone was so interested in heading out to fast food restaurants or eating healthy at home that they forgot this place existed. Until you came along, that is."

Sammy flushed, not wanting to take credit for the success of an entire business. She knew Just Like Grandma's was built on much more than just a few cakes and pies. "I'm sure that's not true."

"And I'm sure it is, and I can't thank you enough for it. I promised myself I would run a successful restaurant. It was what I always wanted to do, and I thought I'd be breaking that promise. Thought I might shut it all down and go get myself a job as a greeter at the discount store. I'm glad you saved me from that fate, Sammy. I'd look terrible in a blue vest."

She just shook her head and laughed, knowing there was no arguing with Helen. "Whatever you say." She popped her pie into the oven, dusted her hands on her apron, and immediately set about making another one.

"I'm heading over to Oak Hills to check out the new boutique that's just opened, if you want to come with me." Kate untied her apron and set it in the hamper to be laundered. "Goodness knows I need some new clothes, maybe something with some lighter weight fabric."

The flow of customers had slowed to a trickle after the dinner rush, at which point the younger girls had pressured Helen into going home and putting up her sore feet. Helen would work all night, otherwise. The trickle, too, had stopped eventually, and the "Closed" sign now hung crookedly in the front door. The rest of Sunny Cove was beginning to shut down for the night as well, with the sign over the pharmacy extinguished and traffic slowing down on Main Street.

Sammy wiped down the counter top, finding one more spot of flour she'd missed. The stuff got all over the place, especially when she was working on pie crusts. It was worth it. An array of strawberry rhubarb, apple, and cherry pies was ready to go out on the table in the morning. "I appreciate it, but probably not. I've got a lot of things I need to work on."

Kate raised an eyebrow. "Like what? Don't tell me you're going to continue working after hours."

She shrugged self-consciously. "Well, maybe. But it's not cake season right now, and I want to get in all the practice I can while I don't have any anxious brides breathing down my neck." As much time as she spent baking for work, it was a passion she had a difficult time putting aside even when she was off the clock.

"Why should you need practice? I saw the cake you did for Chelsea Little, not to mention the one for Andrew Herzog and his wife. You're amazing, Sammy."

Flushing, Sammy shook her head. She'd been very pleased with her work on those two cakes, and the customers had been happy as well. "It's a wonderful sentiment, but there's always some new trend to get ahead of. Every time I get online, there's a new idea popping up. That's what my customers are going to want, too. They're usually not just happy with a traditional cake covered in white roses. They head straight for the internet and have entire idea boards put together before they even talk to me. I'd hate to have to tell them I can't do something." It was something that she thought about a lot. The wealth of information and sharing of ideas was a wonderful thing, but it also meant she had more to keep up with.

"Still, it does seem like you put a lot of yourself into your work. I'd like to see you enjoy yourself sometime." Kate pulled the pins from her bun and let her hair down in long dark waves, shaking them out.

Sammy looked at her, seeing that she still had the energy and eagerness of her youth. Kate hadn't been through any real hard times in life just yet. She hadn't seen her father put in jail for a crime he hadn't committed. She hadn't married a man she thought she loved, only to discover that he'd betrayed her with her best friend. She hadn't had to return to her home town for lack of any other place to go, struggling to find herself again. Sammy didn't feel sorry for herself, but her experiences had left her feeling a little more like spending time alone than running around to boutiques.

"I do enjoy myself," she assured her coworker. "I love what I do so much that I'm practically addicted to it. In fact, I'm running over to Oak Hills as well, but only to buy some new frosting tips." Sammy winked as she dropped her apron in the hamper and turned to the back door, holding it open for Kate.

"Well, just make sure you have fun, and if you ever want to go shopping for something other than baking supplies, you know where to find me!" Kate waved as she got behind the wheel of her sedan and drove off with a smile on her face.

The evening was a beautiful one, even if the heat and humidity were a bit oppressive. Sammy cranked up the radio and bobbed her head along to the music, enjoying just being off her feet for a while with a vent of cool air blasting on her face. Sunny Cove was a small town, and even the "rush hour" didn't put much of a dent on travel time. She would make it to the store in Oak Hills in record time, maybe spend a few minutes looking over new mixers and cutting boards, pick up the frosting supplies she needed, and then head back home for some major cake decorating in her apartment over Just Like Grandma's.

She gave a sigh of happiness as she thought about her apartment. It was small, with just one bedroom, but it was like a sanctuary to her. The place was right over Just Like Grandma's, it had come with the job when she'd returned to Sunny Cove. The pale green walls and white trim always looked bright and welcoming, and the thick walls made for good soundproofing. It was like her own little world up there, and she loved it.

But just as she turned onto the highway that lead to Oak Hills, her Toyota suddenly seemed unwilling to make the trip with her. It spurted and sputtered, making odd noises and slowing down. Sammy stomped the accelerator, suddenly very aware of the line of cars behind her waiting to get on the highway, but the car refused to cooperate. The dashboard lit up in a Christmas display of lights before going dark completely as Sammy managed to yank the car to the side of the road. It rolled to a stop in the grass.

"What the heck?" Sammy had spent a lot of time with her dad when she was a kid, and that occasionally included fixing a car or two. But all she'd ever really done was hand him a wrench or fetch him a cold Coke, and she didn't have a clue what to do about this. She turned off the car and attempted to turn it on again, twisting the key in the ignition. Nothing. "This can't be good. Come on." She tried the key again, but she didn't even get a click.

Sammy sighed and rested her forehead against the steering wheel. It was already getting hot inside the car without any air conditioning, her skin slick with sweat. Not thinking about it, she pressed the button to roll the window down. Of course, that didn't work without any power. She ran over the options in her mind. She hadn't purchased the roadside assistance package on her car insurance, trying to save as much money as possible after she divorced Greg and moved halfway across the country to her hometown. A tow truck was going to be expensive, and then where would she have it towed?

A knock on the window startled her out of her troubled thoughts. Sammy yanked her head up to see a familiar face scowling through the driver's window at her. She pushed the button to roll her window down, but just like everything else on the car, at the moment, it didn't work. With a frustrated sigh, she opened the door.

"Are you all right?" Sheriff Jones asked, watching her carefully. "It's way too hot to be sitting out here in a car." His face was shaded by his wide-brimmed hat, but lines of concern were etched across his forehead.

"I know. I've only been here a couple of minutes. My stupid car quit working." Sammy glared at her blue RAV4. It had carried her thousands of miles, and she'd always loved it for its smooth drive and ample cargo space. Just now, though, she wasn't feeling too grateful.

Jones took the liberty of sitting sideways in the driver's seat and turning the key. Sammy half-expected the car to betray her completely and run like a dream for him, but he didn't get any better results than she had. He nodded, his mouth a straight line. "Might be your alternator."

This knowledge didn't make her feel any better. "What do you think I should do?" She hated feeling like a damsel in distress, but she definitely was.

"Have it towed over to A-1 Auto. Blake works on all the squad cars. And you should be glad you didn't get any further down the road than you did. It shouldn't cost too much for a tow from here. Want me to call it in?" He put a hand on his radio.

Sammy opened her mouth to tell him no thanks, she'd take care of it herself. There was no reason she couldn't use her cell to call a tow truck. But the sheriff seemed so at ease with the situation. "Yeah, that'd be great."

The tow truck arrived shortly, picking up Sammy's Toyota like it was light as a feather and swinging around to head back toward town. Jones offered Sammy a ride, and they followed along behind it to the auto shop. "Since it's after hours, you can just drop the key in the lock box by the door."

Sammy stepped out of the squad car, key in hand. The tow truck was on the far side of the gravel parking lot, beeping noisily to itself as it slowly lowered the Toyota. A-1 Auto wasn't much to look at. A plain white building with two garage bays which had big red letters hand-stenciled across the top of the doorways. An ancient vending machine sat at the corner, humming loudly as it tried to keep up with the summer heat. Numerous cars sat in the lot, most of them looking like they were ready for the junkyard.

Still, the sheriff had recommended this place, and she didn't know of any better options. She dropped her key in the black lock box by the door.

When Jones dropped her off at her apartment a few minutes later, she passed her empty parking spot and headed up the stairs. Sammy opened the fridge to grab a drink and frowned. There was the cake she was supposed to practice on that night, sitting smugly on a plate and covered in plastic wrap. Maybe she should've just gone to the boutique with Kate, after all.

2

EASILY MADE, EASILY BROKEN

The next morning started early, with the scent of coffee, biscuits, and bacon heavy in the air shortly after Sammy arrived at work. People in Sunny Cove had no qualms about having dessert with breakfast, and the pies were already starting to dwindle. Kate wasn't scheduled to come in until lunch time, though, so Sammy focused on serving plates of biscuits and gravy and French toast before she could think about getting any of her baking done.

A young mother and her child sat at a table in the corner. The little girl was happily coloring on her children's menu, her curly pigtails tipping from one side to the other as she studied her work. The mother, however, seemed a little more stressed. She bit her thumbnail as she looked over the menu, looking up and tucking her hand under her other arm when she saw Sammy heading her way.

"What can I get for you ladies today?" Sammy asked with a smile.

The little girl stopped her coloring and grinned. "Mommy promised me she'd bring me here for breakfast, because it's my birthday!"

"Is it? Well that's wonderful! Happy birthday!"

"Thank you! Mommy said I have to enjoy it, because it's the last time we'll be eating out for a long time."

"Lacey, hush!" The mother looked horrified and refused to look Sammy in the eye. "She'll have the birthday cake pancakes with sausage and a cup of milk, please."

Sammy noted it on her pad. "And for you?"

"Um, just a cup of coffee, please."

"Coming right up." Sammy walked back to the kitchen, feeling troubled. But the hectic air of Just Like Grandma's soon took over, and she was caught up in the rush of getting everyone taken care of before it was time to wipe syrup from the tables and sweep crumbs from the floor.

The two diners and her interaction with them returned to her mind as she saw the little girl was done with her pancakes and Sammy prepared to give them their check. She stood behind the counter, holding the ticket in her hand and frowning at it.

"What's the matter? Can't read your own writing?" Helen teased.

"Come here." Sammy led her back to the kitchen, where the customers wouldn't overhear, and explained the situation. "I feel so bad. The mom didn't get any food for herself, and I have a feeling it's because she can't afford it. I didn't want to just give her a meal on the house, because I wouldn't want her to feel like a charity case."

Helen took the ticket and looked at it. "Birthday cake pancakes, huh?"

"It's her birthday, apparently."

Her boss smiled as she inked a large X over the top of the order. "Pancakes are free for birthday girls, Sammy."

"Just one of the many reasons I love you, Helen." She gladly delivered the ticket for only the price of the cup of coffee, assuring the mother that it was absolutely the correct amount.

On her lunch hour, when Kate had arrived, Sammy headed out the back door and down the street to A-1 Auto. She crunched past rusty trucks and old cars to the building. The garage bay doors were open, loud rock music blaring out from them. She could see her Toyota had been pulled inside. "Hello?"

"Hi, there!" A man in a blue jumpsuit popped up from under the hood of an old Chevy. His short hair was spikey with sweat. With his slim face and bright blue eyes, he didn't look like a typical grease monkey. "What can I do for you?"

"This is my car!" she shouted over the music.

The mechanic hurried across the room to hit the volume button on a large stereo. "Sorry about that. You said you own the Toyota?"

"That's right. I'm Sammy Baker."

"Blake Hendricks." He held out his hand to shake hers, but he pulled it back when he realized it was covered in grease. He wiped it off on a rag but didn't offer it again. "Do you want the good news or the bad news?"

Sammy refrained from groaning out loud. Why did their have to be bad news? "Just hit me with it."

19

"Your alternator is bad. It's not a difficult fix, but it will cost a few hundred dollars. The bad news is that I can't pick one up locally. I have to order it."

"How long will that take?"

Blake shrugged. "A couple of days, but once I get it in it won't take long to actually put on the car."

Sammy scowled over her shoulder at her car, still mad at it for breaking down on her and leaving her at the mercy of Sheriff Jones, whom she imagined was more than happy to play the knight in shining armor. "Is there anything else wrong with the car that you could see? I mean, do you think it's worth fixing?"

"Oh, absolutely!" The mechanic stepped away from the old Chevy to give the Toyota a pat on the hood. "You've got a lot of mileage left in this vehicle. Most of these Toyota can rack up hundreds of thousands of miles before they're ready to call it quits. Your interior is still in great shape, too."

Sammy raised her eyebrows, surprised to hear anyone praise her vehicle. She'd always liked it, but it wasn't a Mercedes or anything. "Well, thanks."

"You're very welcome. You know, a lot of people don't like to fix up their vehicles anymore. They treat them like something they can just throw away, because it's easier to just head to the dealership and shell out the money for that new car smell." The smile he had while praising her vehicle faded into a frown. "It's really a shame, you know."

"Yeah. I guess you're right." She'd never really thought about what a waste that would be, but Sammy had never been the type to get a new car. The Toyota was only the second car she'd ever owned, and even it had been used when she'd bought it. "Well, I guess just let me know when you have it finished. I work just down the street at Just Like Grandma's, so that's probably the easiest way to get a hold of me during the day."

"Oh, I know that place." Blake patted his flat stomach. "Best burger in town, not to mention the pie!"

Sammy returned to work, feeling disappointed. Most of the time she didn't need to worry about a car. She only had to walk down the stairs to be at work, so it wasn't as though she had a commute to worry about. In a way, that made her problem much easier to deal with than it would be for most people. Still, she didn't like the idea of being caged in by the lack of a vehicle, and a small town like Sunny Cove had very little in the way of public transportation.

Restless after work, Sammy headed off for another walk. She passed the other local shops, seeing them all in much more detail now that she wasn't speeding by in a vehicle. Pedestrians said hello as she passed them on the sidewalk, and she noticed just how many people rolled through the intersections without fully stopping. It was hot, but at least they were past the blazing heat of July.

Sunny Cove Services, located in the old theater building, was just around the corner, and she stopped in to see how things were going. Sammy had helped establish the business as a way for disabled folks to learn life skills and find meaningful work. Austin, her inspiration, was there to greet her at the door.

"Sammy! I haven't seen you in forever!" He snatched her up in a bear hug that would've been completely unprofessional in any other work setting.

"I know. I'm sorry," she gasped when he set her down. "I've been so busy. How are things going here?" She glanced around the large room, pleased to see that people were busy working with the industrial shredders that formed a large part of the jobs for the workforce.

Austin's dark eyes shone with excitement. "There's a nice old lady who came in to show us how to sew our buttons back on if they fall off. I poked myself with a needle. Look!" He held up a bandaged finger. "Did you know the ancient Greeks used honey on their cuts?"

Sammy couldn't help but smile. Austin was always rattling off a random fact from one of the numerous documentaries he liked to watch, and Sammy was fairly certain he'd read an entire set of encyclopedias. "I didn't know that."

"Sammy, darling!" Sonya McTavish, a tall woman who could've been a supermodel, came floating out from a side door. She owned the building and had been happy to give Sunny Cove Services a good deal on rent, and most recently she'd stepped in as manager. Sonya waved her manicured fingernails in greeting. "It's so good to see you, and I'm glad you stopped by. One of the stoves has stopped working."

"Oh, that's not good." She followed Sonya over to the small kitchen, where Sammy sometimes taught cooking lessons. "When did that happen?"

"Just the other day. I popped a birthday cake in for one of the guys—nothing special like you make, just from a mix—and it came out as a pan of batter. I told Rob, and he said he'd call you."

Sammy nodded. Rob Hewitt, a local lawyer, had done a lot to help Sammy get this place established. "He probably just hasn't had a chance to call me yet. But I've got the name of a woman who has all sorts of kitchen equipment in a storage barn. I'll bet we could get a good price." Sammy had spoken with Rosina Fitzgerald when she'd been thinking of opening her own bakery. The woman had owned all sorts of restaurants, and she never got rid of anything.

Sonya flicked her fingers through her long waves of dark hair. "For a non-profit agency like this, I bet I can get it for free. Just give me her number and I'll take care of it."

Austin caught her again when she was headed for the door. "Hey, Sammy! Can you give me a ride to the library?"

She nodded, more than happy to help out her friend, but then Sammy remembered that she wasn't currently capable of giving anyone a ride. Not even herself. "I'm sorry, Austin. My car's in the shop."

"Okay. I'll ask Uncle Mitch."

"Tell him I said hi. And make sure you stay out of trouble, okay?" It was a running joke between the two of them, since she'd first met Austin when he was getting arrested all the time for petty theft. He had stayed on the right side of the law once Sammy befriended him and made sure he had gainful employment.

"I will!" he promised enthusiastically.

She left, but she wasn't quite ready to go home yet. Sammy ambled on past the church and ended up at Holland Motors. Unlike A-1 Auto, the cars crowded onto the asphalt lot were shining brightly in the sun. Balloons and flags waved in the breeze, their brilliant colors meant to attract the attention of anyone who hadn't already noticed all the gleaming vehicles. On an impulse, Sammy began wandering through the rows.

"Hi there!"

Sammy bit back a scream as she turned around. The man who'd come up behind her was wearing a suit, and he didn't seem to mind the heat. His steely hair was combed back carefully over a wide forehead, and he grinned from ear to ear as he jingled the coins in his pockets. "What can I do for you?"

"I'm just looking around," Sammy explained, still recovering from the scare. "My car is in the shop."

"Jimmy Holland!" the man practically shouted, sticking out his hand.

Sammy shook it, noticing how soft and clean it was. "Sammy Baker."

"All right, Sammy Baker. Now what kind of vehicle are you looking for? An SUV for hauling the kids around? A convertible so you can let your hair down and cruise down the highway?"

"Oh, um, no. I'm really not sure. Like I said, I'm just looking. I wasn't even considering a new car, but then the alternator went out on my car, so I'm on foot for the moment." She squinted against the gleam of a cute red coupe.

"You can't have that! No ma'am! And you know, the older the car, the fewer the safety features you have. Have you had your airbags inspected lately?" He jingled his pockets again, anxious for her answer.

Sammy stiffened. She hadn't even thought about something like that. "My car isn't really that old."

"Old enough it's breaking down! Tell you what: Why don't you pick something out and take it for a little spin around the block?" He grinned, practically pushing her toward another row of cars.

"Look, I really don't have the time right now. I'll be sure to check back with you if I make up my mind." She turned away and headed out of the lot. Jimmy Holland wasn't the stereotype of a car salesman, with a plaid jacket and gold rings, but he might as well have been. He was incredibly pushy, and Sammy didn't feel like being pushed into anything.

3

A SLICE OF SUMMER

The next day, as Sammy got out of bed and stretched, she thought again about her frosting tips. She had a decent stock of baking supplies, of course. It'd been her hobby for quite a while before it'd become her career. Still, it was driving her crazy that she couldn't practice some of the new techniques she'd seen online.

That was it! She didn't need to find a way over to Oak Hills to get what she needed. She could just order everything online. Still in her pajamas, Sammy opened her laptop on the kitchen table and started searching. The biggest challenge was to decide which site she should go through. Sammy compared reviews, shipping costs, and available products. There was far more at her fingertips with just a few clicks than if she'd gone to the kitchen store over in

Oak Hills, and before she knew it she was adding piping bags, a new frosting knife, and several pots of food coloring to her cart. The receipt promised it would be there faster than she'd get her car back.

Sammy had forgotten how exciting it was to shop online and was getting so caught up in the process that she hadn't been paying any attention to the time. She was about to be late for work! Sammy shut the laptop and dashed through the shower, throwing on her clothes and thundering down the stairs.

"Congestion on the freeway?" Helen joked.

"Sorry," Sammy muttered. She felt bad, even though she knew her boss didn't really mind. Sammy put in enough extra hours without being asked that Helen wasn't going to judge her for being a couple of minutes late. Still, she'd taken quite a liking to Helen, and she didn't want to disappoint her in any way. She quickly tied on a clean apron and pushed through the door to the dining room.

She nearly bumped into Kate, who was holding a coffee carafe in each hand. "Oh, good," she said once she'd backed away and balanced the heavy coffee pots. "I'm glad you're here. There are only two pies left, and I highly doubt they'll last long."

"Where did they all go?" Sammy mused as she walked over to the baked goods table. Sure enough, two lonely pies sat in the middle of the white emptiness of the tablecloth. "I'm getting picked clean every day!"

"Nothing you can really complain about, right?" Kate said with half a shrug and a smile. "At least you know people love it."

"Yes, and that's wonderful, but I'm out of ingredients! I'll have to run out to that produce stand on Hoffman Road to get more." She started to untie her apron again, knowing the pies couldn't wait, but she smacked her forehead and stopped before she ever made it back into the kitchen. "But I can't do that, because I don't have a car. Darn it!"

"I can take you out there."

Sammy hadn't even noticed the man sitting at the counter. Rob Hewitt was dressed in a pale gray suit with a green shirt that matched his eyes, finishing off a plate of steak and eggs.

"You don't have to do that, Rob. I don't want to inconvenience you, and I know you're busy." He was probably the most prominent lawyer in town.

He waved his fork in the air in dismissal. "I don't mind. I've got a couple hours before I have to be at the courthouse, and it'll do me some good to get out into the country air for a minute."

"If you're sure, that'd be great."

A few minutes later, Sammy was climbing into the passenger seat of Rob's luxury sedan. The butter-soft leather seats and high-end stereo made her glad she was riding in his car instead of vice-versa. She'd be embarrassed for him to see her cloth upholstery and factory radio if he was used to this sort of elegance. "I really do appreciate this," Sammy said genuinely, buckling her seatbelt.

"Any time. What's going on with your car?" Rob buckled his own belt before starting the engine with a push of his thumb. It whirred to life, humming quietly to itself under the hood.

Sammy briefly explained what was wrong with the Toyota, leaving out the part about Sheriff Jones coming to her rescue. That still embarrassed her for some reason. "Anyway, it'll be a few days. I don't even think about how convenient it is to have a car most of the time, but I'm sure missing it right now. I even walked down to the dealership to see what they have."

Rob glanced away from the road to give her a serious look. "Not Holland Motors?"

She shrank down a little in her seat. "Well, yeah. It's the only dealership in town, isn't it?" Every now and then, someone would park a vehicle for sale in the empty lot near the car wash, hoping some kid would come along and buy it, but that was about the extent of their options.

The lawyer shook his head as he turned to go out of town. "I wouldn't deal with them if I were you. Jimmy Holland is notorious for overcharging on those vehicles. He's all about profit."

"Isn't that the goal for anyone running their own business?" Sammy countered.

"Sure, and I have to say I wouldn't want to work for free myself. But there's a difference between making a little money and shaking people down for all they're worth. Customers get excited about the prospect of a new car, and old Jimmy can see them coming. You didn't hear this from me, but I've been told that Jimmy sometimes withholds his employees' paychecks." Rob shook his head.

"That's terrible! Why would he do a thing like that?"

Rob shook his head and put one hand up helplessly. "Same reason he jumps out to talk to customers before the salesmen who work for him get a chance: money. He wants it all to himself."

Sammy felt as though she'd been chastised by an older brother. "But what else am I supposed to do if I decide to get a new car?"

"If you're really dead set on it, then you need to go to one of the bigger cities."

"Like Oak Hills?" Sammy thought of the frosting tips at the kitchen store but then reminded herself she'd be getting them in the mail.

"Even bigger. The bigger the better. There are tons of dealerships in places like that, not just one guy who's got the monopoly on the whole town. More buyers, too, which keeps the salesmen motivated to pass on some savings. I've bought a few cars that way, and I'd be happy to take you around and help you negotiate if you're interested."

Sammy had gotten to know Rob a lot better over the last few months, but she still felt strange about accepting such a large favor from him. Still, she didn't want to turn it down completely, in case Blake found something else wrong with her car. "I'll keep it in mind. I'm not sure what I want to do yet. Oh, I stopped in at SCS yesterday." She was glad to change the subject.

Rob smacked the steering wheel lightly with the palm of his hand. "Oh, I was supposed to talk to you about the stove."

"It's okay. Sonya told me. I gave her the number for Rosina Fitzgerald, and Sonya's convinced she can finagle some equipment out of her for free." A year ago, Sammy never would've imagined a woman like Sonya McTavish as the kind of person who would be such an asset to a place like Sunny Cove Services.

"I don't doubt she will."

By this point, they had reached the produce stand. Rob pulled over in the grassy lot next to it so they could get out and look at the offerings. The stand was essentially a flatbed trailer with cardboard boxes full of freshly-harvested crops with handmade signs in each of them. She loaded Rob's trunk up with strawberries, rhubarb, and some fresh blueberries that would make amazing muffins. The customers at Just Like Grandma's were going to be very happy.

4

PRETTY AS A PIE...OR CAKE

ammy sat in her apartment the next day massaging her feet. Helen had insisted that she not worry about waiting tables, sweeping floors, or washing dishes. She and Kate could take care of that. Helen needed Sammy to catch up on her baking before the customers showed up with pitchforks and torches.

"I don't know what kind of magic you're putting in those pies to make people go so crazy for them," the older woman said with a wink, "but keep right on doing it!"

Sammy had been happy to oblige. She'd spent the entire day in the kitchen, crafting as many pies as possible. She made it more exciting for herself by experimenting with different crust patterns, cutting

35

out different shapes and making them into pieces of edible art. Along with the strawberry rhubarb pies, she made a couple of apple pies and a chocolate pie with a high meringue topping. The blueberry muffins were ready to go for the morning, and Sammy had no doubt they would disappear along with the first couple pots of coffee.

All of that was wonderful and left her feeling extremely accomplished, but that was also why her feet hurt so badly. She sat on her couch, grimacing as she rubbed her thumbs into the bottoms of her feet. She made a mental note to ask Helen for some new anti-stress mats in the kitchen.

The knock on her door was unexpected, and Sammy hopped to her feet without thinking. She immediately sat back down again, but she couldn't exactly answer the door from the couch. Hobbling across the room, Sammy opened the door to find the mailman standing at the top of the stairwell, his arms full of packages.

"Delivery for Samantha Baker," he said, a stream of sweat making its way down the side of her face.

"Oh, no!" Forgetting her foot pain, Sammy immediately began taking boxes out of his arms and stashing them on the kitchen counter. "I'm so sorry!"

The mailman laughed. "There's no need to be sorry. This is my job, after all."

"Yes, but that's a lot of parcels to carry all the way up the stairs!"

He waved off her concerns, but Sammy noticed how he rubbed his arms. "It's really not a problem. People are ordering cat litter and dog food online these days, so these packages weren't that bad. A little awkward, but at least they weren't heavy. And they still weren't as awkward as that giant area rug I delivered on the other side of town last week!" He laughed at his own little joke.

"I don't normally order much online, but my car is out of commission," she explained, still feeling bad. Sammy was the kind of person who put her shopping cart back in the corral so a worker wouldn't have to do it, and she even returned the clothes she'd tried on back to their original racks. Somehow, it hadn't occurred to her that the mailman would have to deal with her online shopping spree. "I've got my car in the shop over at A-1."

The mailman made a sour face, pursing his lips and scrunching his eyebrows together. "I wouldn't recommend using that place, if I were you."

"No?" Sammy had been a little uncertain at first, simply because A-1 Auto looked more like a junk yard than a car shop, but Sheriff Jones had recommended it. Meeting Blake had made her feel much better about the whole thing.

But the postman still wore that dour expression. "No. Blake is a passionate man. He loves cars, and he's been working on them forever. I don't doubt that he knows his stuff, but…" He trailed off, shifting uncomfortably from foot to foot.

"But what?" The conversation was making Sammy nervous. If there was a reason not to have Blake work on her car, then she needed to know.

"Well, he takes forever, for one thing. He never gets the repairs done when he says they're going to be, and sometimes he isn't even at the shop when he's supposed to be. Don't get me wrong. I think Blake is a good guy, but he's not a good businessman. It's probably the alcohol."

Sammy was stunned. Blake didn't seem like the kind of guy who was a big drinker, but she supposed that wasn't necessarily something you could tell from meeting someone once. "I didn't realize."

The mailman nodded. "Oh, yeah. I see his truck parked at the bars all the time, and not necessarily the nicer ones. All hours of the night, too."

Pressing a finger to her lips, Sammy wondered what she was supposed to do. She couldn't exactly go get the vehicle back without it having been fixed. That would mean she'd have to pay another tow bill, and the first one plus the repairs were already going to have to come out of her savings. "I see. I appreciate you telling me."

"Not a problem. There's a guy over in Oak Hills who does a good job. He can do all the foreign cars, too, and the new ones with the computers and stuff. He's expensive, but you know the work is done right." He gave her the name, wished her luck, and told her to have a nice day.

Sammy jotted the name down on the small markerboard on the fridge where she wrote her grocery list, but she wasn't sure yet what she was going to do. It was all getting more complicated the longer things wore on. Everyone had their opinion, and they were more than happy to give it to her. That was both the blessing and the curse of living in a small town.

But for the moment, since all the mechanic shops would be closed, Sammy distracted herself with her newly arrived merchandise. She unpackaged her frosting tips and other baking accessories, putting them in a sink of hot, soapy water so they would be ready to use as soon as she made another cake. The one she'd had in the fridge had gone stale, which was a shame, but it wouldn't happen again. Fun decorating ideas were flooding her brain as she washed and dried her new things.

The final and largest box contained a wall clock and a few organizer baskets that she'd ordered on impulse the other morning. She didn't regret the decision, considering how little she'd done to make this apartment truly hers since she'd moved in. Sammy happily sang to herself well into the night as she baked a new cake, put it into the fridge to cool, and went back online to shop for throw pillows and framed prints. This place was going to look just as pretty as her pies.

5

THE CRUST OF THE MATTER

The phone at the restaurant rang, and Sammy jumped for it. "Thank you for calling Just Like Grandma's. This is Sammy. How can I help you?" she asked hopefully.

"I'd like to place an order to pick up, please."

Sammy wrote down what the customer wanted and told her she could come by to get it in about fifteen minutes. Then she went to the back and took her cell phone out of her purse. No calls. She turned down the ringer and slipped it in her apron pocket, just in case.

"What's the matter?" Kate asked as she refilled the coffee pot. "If you were a nail-biter, I'd think you'd have bitten you fingers down to stubs by now."

"I'm just anxious for a call from the mechanic. My car should be ready today. I told him he could reach me here, but what if he forgot where I told him I worked? Maybe he doesn't have any way of getting a hold of me." Truth be told, she was even more worried after her conversation with the mailman the other day. If Blake was an alcoholic, he might not be doing a very good job of fixing her car. And that also opened up the possibility that he would rip her off or not get her car done on time. She didn't have any specific place she needed to go, but she liked the idea of being *able* to go somewhere.

"Why don't you just walk down there and ask him?" Kate suggested. "I can handle things for a little while."

"Are you sure?" Sammy liked the idea, just because it was driving her nuts not to know what was going on with her Toyota.

"Oh, yeah. We've got enough pie to hold off the mob for a while, and things are relatively slow right now. Go, or else I'm going to start getting upset, too." Kate pointed toward the back door.

Sammy had to smile despite her worries. She and Helen had thought long and hard about hiring another person at Just Like Grandma's. The two of them and Johnny had worked so well together, and it was a dynamic they didn't want to mess up. But Kate was fitting in wonderfully. She worked just as hard as the rest of them, and she helped promote that friendly atmosphere that the restaurant was known for.

Stepping out into the sunshine, Sammy headed down the street. It wasn't a very long walk to A-1 Auto, but she was starting to feel the effects of all this walking. It wasn't the same as standing on her feet while working, and she had a lot more energy than she normally did. Maybe, once this was all over with, she'd try to find a way to incorporate more exercise into her day.

Most of the other pedestrians smiled or said hello as she passed, once again making her appreciate small town life. That wouldn't happen in a big city, where everyone was too busy trying to get where they were going to notice each other. She waved to a deputy passing in his squad car, said hello to a mailman who didn't work her route, and smiled at a young woman working on a display in a store window.

Everyone seemed happy and friendly until she passed the bank. A man came charging out of the door, pressing his cell phone to his ear. He glared at the ground, his free hand balled in a fist. "I can't keep doing this, Jim!" he growled as he shouldered his way down the sidewalk. "The bank is going to call my note in, and they don't care what kind of excuses I give them!"

Sammy dodged around him and turned down the street to the auto shop.

A-1 was a bit of an eyesore against the beautiful day and just around the corner from the downtown shops. Sammy had grown accustomed to this, but what she didn't expect was to find all the garage doors closed. There was no loud music, and no friendly mechanic in sight. She hurried forward to the office door, hoping to find that someone was still around. The hours posted on the door stated that the place should be open, but the door was locked and there was no one in sight.

Frustrated, Sammy pulled out her cell phone and called the number on the door. If she listened hard enough, she could hear the phone ring inside. The number must not have gone to Blake's personal cell, and there wasn't even an option to leave a voicemail.

Sammy scanned the parking lot. Her car was off to the left, but of course she had no way of telling if it'd been fixed or not. She hadn't even brought her spare key, so there was nothing she could do with it.

Kicking an aluminum can that rolled through the parking lot, Sammy stewed over the situation. She'd brought her car here because the place had been recommended, but it seemed like everyone she'd talked to since then thought it was a bad idea. If she'd still been back in New York, she wouldn't have needed to wonder. She'd have taken her car right back to the dealership where she'd bought it, where they serviced everything they sold. Yes, it was a little bit more expensive than the smaller repair places, but at least she knew they were always using certified parts and mechanics. They even kept track of what they'd done to the vehicle and called her when she was coming due for maintenance.

But that just wasn't how things were done in Sunny Cove, a tiny town that people outside the area had never even heard of. They were insulated from the rest of the world in many ways, and that wasn't always to their benefit.

As frustrated as she was, Sammy didn't know what she could possibly do about the missing Blake. She turned around to head back to work when a truck came rushing into the parking lot, bumping over a pothole and screeching to a stop next to the building. A small wake of dust rose in the air behind it, blowing gently toward the line of cars needing repairs.

Blake jumped out of the driver's seat and jogged over to her. His hair was rumpled and the lines from his pillow case were still evident on his face. "I'm sorry I'm late! I had a very late night and I overslept. Come on in." He unlocked the office door and held it open for Sammy.

She frowned to herself, no longer sure what she should even say to the man. She didn't miss the stink of stale alcohol that clung to him. He didn't seem drunk or hung over, but it wasn't a good start.

"I tried to call," she said as they walked into the office. It was a small room with an old metal desk. Cardboard boxes containing auto parts were stacked along one wall, making it a store room as well. "You said my Toyota would be done by today."

Blake opened up a laptop sitting on the desk and turned it on before sitting down in a battered desk chair. He swiped his hand over his face and blinked before jumping back to his feet. "Do you want some coffee?" A coffee pot was perched on a mini fridge in the corner, the glass sides of the carafe stained from numerous brewings. Blake opened a bottle of water and poured it in the top of the machine.

"No, thanks. I've already had some this morning." Her stomach churned nervously, wondering why he wasn't saying anything about the car.

The mechanic quickly scooped the coffee ground into a filter and turned the coffee pot on before returning to his desk. "I definitely need some. I'm exhausted. Anyway, I did order the alternator for your car, and it was supposed to be here yesterday. My parts delivery showed up, but the alternator wasn't in there." He clacked away at the keyboard as he spoke, more deft with it than she would've expected.

"Oh." Sammy's heart joined her stomach, though she couldn't explain why. She shouldn't have that much of an attachment to a hunk of metal on wheels.

"I called them about it, but they didn't get back to me until the very end of the day. They've sent it out special delivery, but it's still going to take a couple days to get here." He turned the computer around for her to see. "This is the part number for the alternator, and they sent me a tracking number as well. I can copy it down for you, if you'd like."

Sammy shook her head. She'd blamed Blake and the rumors she'd heard about him for her car still being down, but that didn't seem to be the case. He could've called her with this information the day before and saved her some worry, but in the end there was no harm done. The smell of booze indicated that the mailman hadn't been wrong about his drinking problem, but at least in her case it hadn't stopped him from doing his job. "That's all right. Just let me know when it gets here."

"Absolutely. Do you have another phone number in case you're not at the restaurant when I call?" He sat poised with a pen and a scrap of paper.

She gave him her cell and a small smile. "Thanks for letting me know."

"Not a problem! I'm sorry this has turned into such a complicated thing." He scratched the back of his head with a hand that still bore grease stains from the previous day's work.

"That's not your fault," Sammy admitted. "I have to say I thought about getting ……..

Sammy turned to leave. She wished the news about her car had been better, but at least she knew what was happening now.

She'd barely gotten outside the building when another car came careening into the parking lot. The hood was red, even though most of the body was white and the passenger side door was black. A large patch of duct tape held the gas door closed, and none of the hubcaps matched. It pulled up behind Blake's truck nearly hitting it. A skinny man covered in tattoos slowly pulled himself from the driver's seat and ambled toward the building as Blake was opening the garage doors.

"Where have you been?" Blake demanded.

"Calm down, man. I'm only a few minutes late."

Sammy tried not to pay attention, but she hadn't yet reached the sidewalk as she crossed the large parking lot. The men weren't exactly being quiet, either. It seemed ironic to her that Blake should get onto someone else for being late when he'd been late himself.

"No, it's Thursday. You were supposed to be here over an hour ago. Darn it, Charlie! I give you a job, and this is how you treat me."

"I don't know why you're complaining. You're the one making all the money."

"Ha." The short laugh from Blake was a sarcastic one. "I wish. And you have to actually show up to work before you can make any money."

Sammy stepped onto the sidewalk and headed back downtown, wishing she hadn't heard any of that. Blake had made her feel much better about having her car there, but once again she felt uncertain.

On impulse, Sammy stopped in at Carly's Cupcakes. It was just across the street from the path she was taking anyway, and it'd been a while since she'd stopped in to see the young baker. In a way, Sammy thought of herself as Carly's mentor, even if Carly didn't always want to take her advice to heart.

"Sammy!" she enthused from behind the counter where she was boxing up an order. "I'll be right with you."

The customer carried out two big boxes of doughnuts a few minutes later, and Carly was beaming. "It's so nice to see you. How are things going?" She pulled two oatmeal cookies from the case and handed one to Sammy.

"Okay, I guess." She explained her problems with her car. "I know it shouldn't be that big of a deal. It's not like I should think of a car as a necessity, and these are the kind of things people have to handle all the time. But it's just driving me crazy! And everyone seems to have an opinion on where I should be taking it to be fixed, or if I should even fix it at all."

Carly shook her head in sympathy. "I understand. I don't like it when my car breaks down, but I'm lucky enough that my dad is a tinkerer. He likes to fix things, and he jumps on the chance to get under a hood."

"That is lucky." Sammy wished she had someone who could do that for her. But her father had passed away a few years ago, and even when she'd been married Greg wasn't much good at mechanical stuff.

"I'm trying to remember where I've heard the name of the mechanic you mentioned, though. It's really familiar, like maybe he used to work somewhere else."

"I just hope he gets the car fixed and back to me. And this is really good, by the way." The oatmeal cookie was chewy and soft with a wonderful buttery flavor.

"Thanks! I've really been trying. Business is picking up a bit, too. I gave the schools some free cookie coupons they could pass out to students for good grades or good behavior, and that's helped business pick up. That lady that was just in here was buying doughnuts for the staff at the elementary school."

Sammy felt a swelling of pride in her chest. She'd decided a long time ago not to think of Carly as her competition. They had different styles and tastes when it came to baking, and their businesses just weren't the same. Carly had even shown Sammy a lot of support when she'd considered opening a bakery of her own, something that surely would've affected Carly's business a little more than Just Like Grandma's did.

"I'm really happy for you. What about new cars? Have you heard anything about Holland Motor?"

Carly ate the last bite of her cookie and chewed thoughtfully. "I can't think of anything specific, but did you see that little red car they had up at the front of the lot? So cute! I think one of the salesmen has been driving it every now and then, too, because I've seen it around town. I don't really need a new car, but I promised myself I wouldn't do anything like that until I have paid off my credit card debt."

"That's a good idea, and you should stick with it. Well, I'd better get going. I'm working today." Sammy bid her friend goodbye and turned to the door.

Carly snapped her fingers just as Sammy reached for the handle. "That's where I've heard Blake's name before. He used to work at Holland Motors. It's been quite a while. Sorry, that's probably not very relevant, but it was going to drive me crazy until I figured it out."

"I understand. I'll see you!" Sammy headed back to Just Like Grandma's. She'd wasted a little bit of time by stopping in at Carly's Cupcakes, but she was glad she did. It was nice to just stand around and talk with someone without them giving her life advice. Carly was a great girl, and she always had a smile on her face. Sammy pasted one on her own face as she walked in the back door at work, determined not to let the delay in her car repairs get to her.

6

A FINGER IN EVERY PIE

The next morning, Sammy couldn't stop thinking about the little red coupe Carly had mentioned. She'd seen it when she was at the dealership talking to Jimmy Holland, and it'd definitely caught her eye. She could see herself whizzing around town with the windows down. The Toyota had been a more practical purchase, something she'd envisioned would help her haul supplies for her charity work. It would even be a good vehicle for any future children she might have.

But that had been when she was still married to Greg, and before she'd realized the two of them were never going to get that far in life. Maybe Sammy deserved a little something special, something that didn't speak of practicality and discipline. She didn't have a car payment on the Toyota. Her rent for the

54

apartment was taken directly out of her check from Helen, but even that wasn't much since it'd come as part of her employment package. The Toyota was reliable and practical, but the red coupe was flashy and cute.

She was only scheduled for a half a day of work, a luxury now that they had Kate working full-time. Sammy tried to keep her mind focused on her job, but it was difficult. The more she thought about it, the more she wanted that car.

Leaving work promptly at noon, Sammy headed straight upstairs to her apartment. She pulled up her budgeting spreadsheet on her computer, where she kept track of her bills and her paychecks. Her organization skills had always bothered her ex-husband, who thought she was making too much effort to track every dollar, but Sammy liked being able to sit down and examine all the numbers at once. She checked her monthly budget as well as the money she had in savings. She looked up the value of her RAV4. She pulled up the cute red car on the dealership's website so she could figure out a value for it as well. She calculated what the monthly payment should be. By the time she left her apartment, she felt fully armed with information.

Walking across town, Sammy rehearsed what she would say when she got there. She already knew just how pushy Jimmy Holland could be, just like any other car salesman. She wasn't going to let them push her into anything she didn't want, and she wasn't going to accept a higher payment than what she'd already decided on. She knew what her credit score was, and she knew the value of the car. It would all work out.

But when she reached the dealership, Sammy started to wonder if the entire town was avoiding her. A-1 Auto had been closed when she'd showed up the previous day, and now the dealership seemed to be as well. No assertive salesmen came rushing out to grill her about what type of vehicle she was looking for. The colorful banners hung limply from the light poles, with no breeze to make them snap and wave. Even the balloons tied to the antennas had lost some of their air, and they bumped sadly along the hoods of the cars.

Sammy sighed. Fate didn't seem to be working for her when it came to vehicles. She walked up to the sales office to find the door locked and the lights out. Someone had taped a piece of printer paper to the door with "Sorry, closed" written hastily in pen.

She tried to think positively as she headed back downtown. Sammy told herself that this was just God's way of telling her she didn't need that vehicle, even though she knew she could afford it. Or maybe there was some other reason for her not to buy it. She didn't really know anymore. It was a good thing she liked her job so much, or else this was really going to get her down.

When she walked into the back door of Just Like Grandma's, though, she noticed that everyone else was already down. Kate and Helen were out in the dining area, and all the customers were speaking quietly. The entire place seemed to have a somber tone to it, and Sammy knew it had nothing to do with her car problems.

"What's going on?" she asked as Helen stepped up to the cash register.

The older woman sighed. "I wish I could tell you that I didn't know, Sammy. At one point in time, this little town was the safest place you could possibly live. Everyone knew everyone, and if you did something wrong you'd have all your friends and neighbors getting onto you." She punched the numbers into the machine, looking suddenly much older.

"I don't like the sound of that."

"You shouldn't. Jimmy Holland was found dead last night. They think it was a hit and run. How ironic."

Sammy stood there for a long moment, absorbing the news. She'd been so selfish when she'd found out the dealership was closed, because it meant she couldn't get the new car she'd wanted. She'd never thought about what someone else might be going through. Poor Jimmy Holland. And what about his family? Did he have a wife? Children? "Wow."

"I know. Seems like it happened while he was crossing the street. I'll have to have a talk with Alfie about putting in more stop signs or increasing their patrols. People don't pay any attention to the speed limits anymore, even in town." She finished her transaction and left the counter to give the customer their receipt.

Sammy went back into the kitchen. She wasn't scheduled to work any more that afternoon, but there was something therapeutic about baking that she just couldn't resist. She pulled a flat of strawberries out of the cooler and began chopping off the stems.

"What are you doing in here?" Kate asked as she came in from the dining room.

"I don't know what else to do with myself," she admitted. "My plans for this afternoon were, shall we say, thwarted. I was going to buy a new car."

"Oooh." Kate picked up a stack of napkins and began rolling silverware. "I heard about that, but it's not like I can avoid it. Everyone's talking about it. People sure do like to gossip around here."

In a way, Sammy wanted to avoid that gossip. But she was a naturally curious person, and she wanted to know the details. "Have you heard any details? Any suspects?"

"Not a one," Kate replied. "It happened late at night, and the guys Holland was hanging out with said they weren't with him anymore."

Sammy frowned as she topped the remainder of the strawberries and put them in a colander so she could rinse them off. "Interesting. In a place like this, I think of everyone as seeing what their neighbors are doing. There's always someone around. But this one has no eyewitnesses, and no suspects. To be honest, I'm just glad I wasn't the one to find the body."

"Yes, I've heard about all your escapades with that!" Kate said with a laugh. "I'm sorry. It's not like it's funny. I think I'm just looking for a reason to smile. It doesn't sound like the incident was a malicious one, but it still makes me feel a little nervous."

"I don't blame you." Sammy set the strawberries aside and began chopping rhubarb. "I hate to think we might get used to these sorts of things happening in Sunny Cove, but it's like it's becoming less and less of a surprise."

The two women worked together for a while in silence, with only the sounds of Sammy's knife and the silverware Kate was working with. Eventually, Kate pulled in a deep breath to speak. "So, are you going to do anything about it?"

"Do anything about what? The car?"

"No, about Jimmy Holland. I know you've helped solve other cases. Maybe you can figure out what happened to him." Kate put the last of the silverware rolls in a bussing tub and began working on the dirty dishes.

Sammy frowned down at the long stalks of rhubarb. "I haven't really thought about it much. I mean, I'm curious. I think anyone would be. But I'm not sure I want to get involved."

"How come? From what I hear, you're good at it." Kate scraped several plates into the trash and then plopped them in a sink of hot, soapy water.

The compliment was a genuine one, but it made Sammy feel strange. Just how many people were talking about her and the help she'd given in previous cases? Had Sheriff Jones said something, or was this just another product of the local rumor mill? What did it mean for her if she was 'good at' figuring out mysteries? "We'll see. There might not really be anything I can do. Heck, I can't even get to the corner store quickly right now, what with no car. Who knows when my Toyota will be fixed?"

She tried to avoid talking about it for the rest of the day, but it was impossible not to think about it. When she'd set several pies and a cobbler on the bakery table in the dining room, she called it a day and went upstairs.

As much as she thought she might be able to stay out of Jimmy Holland's death, she was already beginning to understand that just wasn't realistic. She wanted to know what happened, and it seemed she did have a knack for such things.

She sat at her kitchen table with a notebook and a pencil and began making a list. She tapped the eraser against her lip, trying to think about who would do such a thing. A customer who'd been ripped off? Possibly, if they felt they'd been gypped out of a lot of money or got a lemon. But how likely would it be for a customer of Jimmy's to just happen along and see him crossing the street? Perhaps more likely in a small town like this one. Sammy added it to the list.

Who else? What if there was no motive at all, but someone had genuinely hit Jimmy by accident? That was perfectly plausible, but then why wouldn't they have called the police? Someone with a record, who couldn't afford another stain on their record, might have thought it a better idea to drive off. Just how many people like that lived in Sunny Cove? Still, Sammy wrote that on the next line.

She came up with a few other ideas, searching for any type of person who might be angry with Jimmy Holland. She didn't know the man well, and that didn't make it any easier. But she added several more ideas to her idea log, including a former lover, a possible business partner, and an old friend who had a quarrel with him. They were all just vague ideas, since she didn't know anything about the man's love life, business associations, or friendships.

Her mind continually returned to a very real possibility that she didn't like. Blake Hendricks had told her, when she'd first talked to him about fixing her car, that he thought too many people chose to buy new vehicles instead of fixing up the old ones. Was he angry with Holland for stealing business from him? And Carly had mentioned that Blake used to work for Holland Motors. That left room for all sorts of problems between the two of them. She imagined a massive fallout between the two of them, ending in a screaming match where they both vowed to get revenge on each other.

It was dramatic and over-the-top, the kind of thing you'd find in a crime novel but not real life. Still, Sammy knew that Blake was a top suspect. Whether the police knew it or not was a different matter. Now, she just needed a plan to find more clues.

7

PITY PIE

ammy was prepared. She'd hardly had any sleep the night before, although she hadn't been spending the night making lists. She already knew what she had to do, or at least how she would get started. It was now her job—as far as she was concerned—to find the connection between Jimmy Holland and Blake Hendricks.

It wouldn't make sense to go talk to Blake just yet. He was supposed to call her when he'd fixed her vehicle, and it only made sense to be patient and wait for that. She couldn't exactly talk to Jimmy, either, since he was dead. But he did have mourning coworkers, and that seemed as good a reason as any to go and visit the dealership.

The problem was finding the time. Sammy, just like the rest of the workers, had a scheduled lunch hour. But that was really only good on paper, because they didn't always get to leave right on time depending on the demand of the customers. Usually, they didn't even get to sit down.

And today was certainly one of those days. The Radical Grandmas were back in, but this time they weren't coordinating for a charity fundraiser. They'd brought their grandchildren and godchildren in with them, and the group took up an entire corner of the restaurant.

"Aren't they just darling?" beamed Viola Hampshire as she pressed her hands together and watched two small girls fighting with each other in a booth. "I promised all the children we would take them over to the library for story hour after this. I wanted to get some good food in their tummies beforehand, though, so they wouldn't be whining."

Sammy noticed with a grimace that the children seemed to be getting far more food on the floor than in their tummies, but it wasn't her place to say so. "I'm sure they'll enjoy that."

Agnes Miller tugged on her sleeve and pointed out her numerous grandchildren, rattling off their names. Sammy hoped she wasn't expected to remember them all, because there were an awful lot of them ranging from a tiny tot who could barely walk to a bored teenager. "We ladies spend so much time together, we thought it would be a good idea to get the kids together, too. We figured they're sure to be just as good of friends as we are. That reminds me, Viola, I was thinking we could bring them all to the movies when we're done at the library."

"What's playing?"

The other woman shrugged as though it really didn't matter. "I have no idea. But you know kids, they like anything on a screen, especially if you put popcorn in front of them."

Sammy refilled drinks and made a mental note to give those tables and chairs a thorough wipe down once the group was gone. She loved the Radical Grandmas and the work they did for the community, but three old ladies who dabbed the corners of their mouths with their napkins were much easier to clean up after than a whole gaggle of children. As she brought another set of crayons to the table, Sammy couldn't help but think of that one little girl who'd come in for birthday cake pancakes with her mother. She hoped they were doing all right.

On the other side of Just Like Grandma's, Andrew Herzog had brought in some suits to dine with him. "I'm telling you, the food here is the real deal. It's all made by hand in the back, not zapped in a microwave like they do at other places. It's real down-home cooking, and you can expect that kind of mentality all over Sunny Cove." As a land developer, Andrew was probably trying to schmooze these guys into investing in some building project. He was notorious for sticking his nose in every business deal he caught wind of, trying to sell ugly architectural plans or tear down local historical sites in favor of new developments.

Sammy wondered what he was up to this time, although she'd come to realize he wasn't really such a bad guy. "What can I get for you gentlemen today?" She took their orders back to the kitchen, knowing she would probably hear soon enough what Andrew had up his sleeve.

Heather Girtman, Sammy's old friend from high school, came in and took a seat at the counter. She'd dyed the tips of her black hair bright blue, and she had the fingernails to match. Heather was a good person at heart, but she wasn't very good at staying out of trouble most of the time. Things were getting a little better now that she'd started going to church with Sammy.

"Hey," Heather said shyly after she'd ordered a grilled cheese. "Are you going to that singles mixer at the church?"

"I haven't even thought about it," Sammy admitted. In fact, her life had been so full between the café and helping out at Sunny Cove Services that she hadn't made much time for anything else. "I'm not sure it's really my thing. I'm not even sure I want to meet other singles."

"You should. It'd be good for you to get out."

That was probably true. "I'll think about it."

"I get it." Heather tapped the counter as though she'd just discovered something. "You're already dating someone, but you don't want to say anything."

"No, I'm not!" Sammy said with a laugh.

Heather shook her finger at Sammy. "You know how tongues wag in this town. Everyone did see you and Sheriff Jones dancing together at Chelsea Little's botched wedding just a couple of months ago. Could that have anything to do with it?"

Sammy's face reddened. She'd had a wonderful time with Jones as her 'date,' even though the entire thing had been a farce they'd put together to catch a criminal. "We're just friends."

Heather raised one dark eyebrow. "If you say so."

By the time Sammy had caught up enough on waiting tables and had made sure the baked goods table wouldn't go empty in the next couple of hours, her feet and her head were both hurting. She wasn't sure she was up to a visit to the dealership, but she knew if she didn't go she would regret it. How else would she ever figure out the truth behind Jimmy Holland's death? In Sammy's mind, he was going to be the world's greatest unsolved mystery until she got to the bottom of it.

Taking a strawberry rhubarb pie and transferring it to a box, she tied a ribbon around it and headed out the back door. The walk outside refreshed her head and her body, even with the heat. The excitement of making headway on her case didn't hurt, either.

Holland Motors was open, but Sammy didn't wait around in the parking lot for someone to come out and start selling her a car. She walked straight into the office, prepared to give them the pie as her way of offering her condolences.

Off to the right of the entryway was a large showroom. Several cars and trucks, each gleaming under the lights, had been put on display with big, brightly colored signs that assured their potential buyers just how safe the vehicles were and what a good deal the new owners would be getting. A large waiting room with overstuffed chairs and a stack of magazines was parked right in the middle of this display.

Right in front of Sammy was a massive gray desk. It, too, was covered in sales information in the form of flyers and brochures. The desk was big enough that it nearly obscured the woman sitting behind it, but Sammy recognized her anyway. It was the young mother who'd brought her daughter in for birthday cake pancakes. She immediately felt another pang for her, wondering what was going on in her life that she couldn't even afford her own breakfast.

"Hi," she said apprehensively, wondering if the woman recognized her as well. "I'm here on behalf of Just Like Grandma's. We heard about what happened to your boss, and we wanted to offer our sympathy. If there's anything we can do, please let us know." She set the box on the counter.

The woman smiled, a spark of remembrance in her eyes as she pressed her lips together. "That's very kind of you."

"It's strawberry rhubarb, which is quite a hit right now. If there's anyone who has allergies or something, I can always make another dessert and bring it over."

The receptionist held the box in her hands as though holding something precious. "It'll be just fine. And that's very kind of you. I don't think anyone else has done something like this."

Sammy wasn't surprised, considering the kind of reputation Jimmy Holland had. "I'm happy to do it. Also, I hate to ask, but are you guys fully open today? There was a car I was interested in."

As though he'd been lurking somewhere behind the desk, just waiting for someone to say the right words, a man appeared through an office doorway with a big smile on his face. He was young, with dark hair and a very professional-looking suit. Sammy nearly took a step back as she recognized him as the same man who'd nearly run into her as he was coming out of the bank the other day, having an angry conversation on the phone. "Of course we are! What vehicle are you looking at?" He escorted her back out onto the lot, graciously holding the door. "I'm Eric, by the way." He stuck out his hand.

She shook it. "That little red coupe over there." She'd spotted it as she walked toward the office, but it was hard not to. The sparkly red would catch anyone's eye.

"Ah, yes. A real beauty. That's the newest Honda, and it's a wonderful ride. I drove it for a day, and it was hard to go back to my own car. It's got all the safety features you could possibly want, leather interior, sunroof, rear camera, GPS, the works." He walked next to her toward the vehicle without pushing her toward it the way Jimmy Holland had done.

Sammy had to wonder what had changed in this man between his visit to the bank and his current workday. Maybe this was just his happy, customer service-oriented attitude he always projected when he was dealing with a potential buyer, or he'd just been having a particularly terrible day when he'd been at the bank. Either way, he was the kind of person Sammy felt instantly comfortable with. "I have to be honest with you. I was looking at it about a week ago. I hadn't really thought about buying a new car, but my current one is in the shop. It's taking a lot longer to get fixed than I had originally planned, and I happened to stop in and it caught my eye."

"Where are you having it worked on?" Eric stopped in his tracks and looked at her seriously.

"A-1 Auto." She watched his face carefully.

Eric tightened his lips and nodded. "There's your problem. He's not the best guy for the job, most of the time. He worked here for a while before Jimmy fired him, and he ended up starting his own business."

Ah ha! There was some animosity between the two, just as Sammy had suspected. She wanted to ask why Blake had been fired, but this didn't seem like the right moment. "I see."

"Now, you had already looked at this car before. Was there another salesman who was helping you?"

She gritted her teeth together, giving him an uncomfortable look. "Actually, it was Jimmy."

That information was enough to make him wave off the idea, and he resumed their walk toward the Honda. "I see. Well, we won't worry about that then. I just didn't want to take over if…. Frankly, he probably wasn't going to give you a very good deal anyway."

Sammy noted that he didn't seem all that concerned that his boss was dead, but neither had the receptionist. Even the gossip about Jimmy's death at the restaurant hadn't lasted all that long, with the conversation quickly turning back to local sports and weather. Interesting. "We hadn't talked much about figures," she admitted.

"That's okay. We can get you all taken care of."

Before she knew it, Eric had her in the driver's seat, pointing out all the controls, safety features, and even the cupholders. He knew the vehicle like the back of his hand. "It's a great little car. If you have a long commute to work, you'll save a ton of money on gas, too."

Sammy had to laugh. "All I have to do to go to work is walk down the stairs. I live and work in the same building."

Eric smiled as he leaned against the doorframe. "Then you really save a lot on gas!"

They took the car for a spin around the block, testing out the air conditioning as well as the sunroof. The salesman turned on the stereo and cranked it up, demonstrating what great speakers the car came with, even straight from the factory. His cell phone chirped in his pocket numerous times, but he always glanced at the screen and put it away. "You'll make everyone in town jealous with this baby."

She blushed, knowing that wasn't her goal at all. "I'm not worried about that. I just thought I might do something nice for myself."

"And you should!" he encouraged as they pulled back into the dealership. Eric directed her to park the car alongside the building instead of back up at the front corner of the lot. "Everyone deserves something nice once in a while. Let's go into my office, and we can talk numbers."

As Sammy followed him back inside and around the receptionist's desk, Sammy saw several pictures of the little girl who'd ordered the birthday cake pancakes. It made her wonder about the woman's salary. Working in a big, nice place like this seemed like the sort of job that would earn a decent amount. Someone else's financial problems weren't her business, but it was so hard for her to let go of the image of that woman ordering nothing but coffee.

Eric seated her in a cushy chair across from his desk and logged into his computer. "Let's get some of your information so we can go ahead and send out your application for financing. It doesn't usually take long, but that way we can be the most efficient. I'm sure you have plenty of things you'd like to do on a pretty day like this."

Sammy appreciated that, and the two of them worked well together as she gave him all the right information. When they started talking about price, Sammy was fully prepared to pull the little notebook out of her purse where she'd written down all the figures she'd researched. She knew she would need to counter the salesman with explaining what her Toyota was actually worth on trade-in and whether or not she actually needed whatever extras they tried to sell her on.

But Eric was shockingly open with her. He turned his computer screen so she could see exactly what he was doing and what he was looking at, and she watched as he pulled up an accurate value for her current car. "Looks like by the time we do a trade-in and a rebate, we should be able to get you a payment right around this figure." He gestured with his cursor to a dollar amount that was actually slightly lower than what she'd planned."

"Wow." Sammy blinked, caught off-guard. "I was really expecting it to be more than that."

He smiled, pleased with himself. "I do my best. Oh, looks like I've got an email here from the bank. And you're approved! I'll get all the paperwork printed up."

Her stomach jumped up into her chest and gave her heart a high-five. "Eric, I'm sorry, but I'm just not sure about this." She'd been thinking about that car non-stop over the last couple of days. She'd done all her research, and the numbers were even better than she'd imagined. Sammy deserved something nice, something new, something that was just hers and a symbol of the new life she'd started since coming back to Sunny Cove. But for some reason, she just couldn't quite commit.

He gazed at her with understanding in his dark brown eyes. "Is there something I can help with?"

She shook her head. "I don't think so. I just...I'm not sure I want to do this."

"Tell you what." He slid the keys across the desk toward her. "Why don't you take the car home for a couple of days. Drive it around, see how it feels, and see how it fits into your life. A car can be just like trying on a pair of jeans in the department store. They look great in the mirror and the perfect lighting, but once you get them home you realize the pockets aren't the right size or the hem doesn't look right with your favorite pair of boots. At least, that's what my wife tells me. I don't really care how my jeans look," he laughed.

Sammy had to smile. "Are you sure it's okay to just take the car like that?"

"Oh, yeah. We do that all the time. We just keep a log in the system of who has the car, and I've got all your information. You're good. Just let me know what you decide." He pulled up a spreadsheet on the computer and added the date and her name to the bottom of the list for the car. Sammy noted that she wasn't the first to borrow the car, and the staff at the dealership had each had their turn with it.

"Okay," she said with a nod, figuring this probably was the best plan of action. It would give her some time to really think about her decision, plus it would be yet another opportunity for her to visit the dealership and try to get a better read on people. That thought suddenly reminded her of why she was here, beyond just getting a new vehicle. "By the way, I'm really sorry to hear about what happened to Mr. Holland. That's just such a terrible thing."

Eric spread his hands on the desk and looked at his fingers. "It's something we're still dealing with, for sure."

She suddenly felt bad for trying to dig into their business. She wanted to grill him on who Jimmy Holland's enemies might be or if he knew any other information that could lead to an arrest, but Sammy had to remember she was just a customer, not a cop. "I know. But thank you for everything you've done today. I'll give you a call soon."

His friendly smile was plastered on his face once again. "Sounds good!"

8
CRUMBLED CRUST

The next day dawned unusually hot, warm enough that it even kept most of the usual customers from coming to Just Like Grandma's. The humidity in the air wasn't helping, either, making everything feel sticky. Everyone began looking forward to the promise of fall in a month or two.

Helen smacked her hand against the air conditioner, squinting at the digital numbers that proclaimed the temperature. "I'm not sure this thing is working."

"I think it's working as hard as it can," Sammy replied, wiping her forehead with the back of her hand. She didn't usually mind the warm weather, but the heat of the day didn't seem good for anything beyond taking a nap. Despite the slow business at the restaurant, she couldn't really do that.

"Do you think I should have someone come in and take a look at it?" Helen fiddled with the dial as she fanned herself with her apron. "Or maybe I should just break down and have a central unit put in. I try too hard to keep this place old-fashioned, I think."

"The heat is getting to your brain, Helen," Kate teased, wiping down the counter where someone had spilled a few drops of coffee. "That old-fashioned feeling is what keeps people coming back. They're crazy about it."

"I think they'd like it better if they weren't melting into their coffee cups. I think I'd like it better, too," the older woman replied sourly, finally leaving the air conditioner alone. "I think I'm going to go stick my head in the freezer."

"I'll join you! Let's see if we can find some ice cream." The two women headed into the back.

Sammy was alone in the dining area, flipping through a newspaper but not really reading it. She felt tired, and the articles in the paper weren't particularly interesting. What little news the press had about Holland's death had already been printed a couple days ago, and they were back to talking about roads that needed to be repaired and speculating over who would run for mayor the next year.

The bell over the door rang, admitting a customer. Sammy looked up to see Sheriff Jones smiling at her as he took off his hat and set it on the counter. "Looks like someone's got a flashy new car. Helen must be paying you too much. I'll have to talk to her about it."

She couldn't help but smile. Alfred Jones was good company, and he always had something interesting to say even if the paper didn't. "You won't go telling her any such thing! I'm not even sure I'm going to keep the car, actually."

"Why not?" He parked himself on a stool, looking surprisingly cool in his uniform. "It's a cute little thing. Can I get a cup of coffee?"

"Yes, and it even drives nicely, and has a sun roof, and there are more cupholders than one person could possibly need. I really do like it. But when it comes right down to it, I just don't know that I want to spend the money." She shrugged as she folded up the newspaper and turned to pick up a coffee carafe. "I'm just borrowing it for right now while I think about it."

"And what about your Toyota?"

Sammy let out a long sigh that seemed to stay in the hot, humid air a little longer than normal. She filled a mug and passed it to him. "There were some issues. There was some sort of mix-up at the parts warehouse, and the alternator didn't come in when it was supposed to. Blake said it should be coming in anytime, but I haven't heard anything from him."

Jones nodded as he slowly stirred a spoonful of sugar into his drink. "He can be a little slow, I admit. But he always gets the job done. We wouldn't keep using him for the squad cars if he didn't. We're not much good if our vehicles aren't reliable."

"I guess that's true, but ever since I took my car over there, I've had tons of people telling me it was a mistake. And it's frustrating not to have a vehicle of my own." She leaned an elbow on the counter.

"I don't know. You seem to be getting around just fine," he said with a slow smile.

"What's that supposed to mean?" She figured he'd seen her hoofing it all over town.

Jones raised his eyebrows and gave a slight shrug. "Oh, you know, that romantic little visit to the

83

produce stand with Rob Hewitt. Everyone's talking about it."

"What?" Sammy hadn't even thought about that since it'd happened. "Are you serious?"

"Sure. I mean, word travels fast when a single man and a single woman are seen out together at a romantic place like a produce stand." He laughed at his own joke.

Sammy rolled her eyes and swatted him gently with the newspaper. "You're terrible." Still, she had to wonder if anyone *was* talking about her outing with Rob and what they thought. She knew they were only friends, and their relationship was usually more about business than anything. It didn't seem fair that she couldn't make a single move without someone noticing. She wasn't all that important. And if that was the case, then why hadn't anyone seen the accident that killed Jimmy Holland?

She was happy to change the subject to something that was less focused on her. "Tell me what you know about Jimmy Holland."

Jones glanced around the dining area. There were only a few people, but apparently that was enough for him. "That's a pretty high-profile case. I don't think I should talk about it."

"Why is it high-profile? It doesn't seem any different to me than any other deaths that happen in Sunny Cove." Sure, Jimmy had owned the only dealership in town, but most people around here were entrepreneurs.

"For one thing, it happened right in the middle of Main Street. Granted, it was the middle of the night, and most people were in bed or at least at home, but still. It makes the case a bit different than when a dead body is found in a home or a business." The sheriff frowned down at his mug, swirling the dark liquid against the white porcelain.

"Do you have any suspects lined up?" she pressed.

"Do you?" he countered. "Sammy, I know you get interested in these things. Everyone does, and everyone's always so curious to know what happened. I think its human nature, and it's perfectly understandable, but the fact is that this is police business."

She frowned at him, surprised at his tone. Sheriff Jones had always been interested in talking over cases with her before. One time, he'd even come up to her apartment and made a list of clues and suspects with her. It seemed strange that he was getting disgruntled about her involvement now, especially when she hadn't yet told him just how involved she'd been. She decided at that moment not to tell him of her suspicions about Blake or the time she'd spent at the dealership. She had no hard evidence, after all. "All right, then. I just thought I'd ask. There wasn't much in the paper, and I hadn't seen you for a while." Sammy busied herself with straightening the row of mugs they kept under the counter, even though they were perfectly fine as they were.

Jones sighed heavily. "I've been busy, and there's practically nothing to go on." He glanced around again before leaning close. "One of my men found a bolt in the street near the scene of the accident, but that's it."

Her attitude changed instantly as she latched onto this piece of information. "A bolt? What kind of bolt? What did it look like?"

But the sheriff sat back on his stool and shook his head grimly. "Just a plain old bolt, nothing special. It could have been there for a long time, and it doesn't necessarily have anything to do with the case. That's precisely what's so frustrating about it, too. You'd think a guy who'd been hit with a car would have some paint that rubbed off on him. I read about a case once where they found the driver based on the imprint of the license plate that was bruised into the victim's skin. But there's just nothing like that in this instance. It sure makes my job hard."

"Don't you have some sort of forensics team you can call on? People who can trace a piece of dust back to where it came from?" Sammy was genuinely interested, but she was still a bit bitter over his reluctance to talk about the case.

"You've been watching way too much television," he grunted.

"I don't really watch any television at all," Sammy reminded him.

"Then reading too much, maybe. But it's never as simple as they make it sound in the media."

"So, this bolt—"

"No." Sheriff Jones held up his hand. "It's just a bolt, a regular old piece of hardware that could have come from anything and anyone at any time. Don't go reading into it." He slugged down the rest of his coffee, put a dollar on the counter and left.

Sammy watched him go, feeling stunned. Jones could occasionally get a little harsh with her when he thought she was putting her nose in a dangerous place, all in the name of solving a mystery. But he'd never been flat out rude like that, and she wasn't sure how to take it.

When Helen came back out to the front with a bowl of ice cream in each hand, setting one in front of Sammy, she frowned at her employee. "What's the matter?"

"Just thinking."

"Tell us everything," Kate said, coming around the counter and occupying a stool across from her. "If there aren't any customers in here gossiping, I don't know what to do with myself."

Sammy smiled at that, because she knew exactly what Kate meant. None of them really ever meant to listen through the grapevine, but it was impossible not to when you worked in a place like this. It was how Sammy knew that Andrew Herzog was working on a new project, how she knew the receptionist at Holland Motors couldn't afford to eat breakfast out, and even how she knew Jimmy Holland was dead. She would've found out eventually through the news or the paper, but the spoken word always seemed to travel faster.

The last customer of the morning cleared out, having polished off a blueberry muffin, and Sammy felt it was safe to talk freely. "I'm probably not supposed to talk about it, but Sheriff Jones was just in here."

"He was? Alfie didn't even bother to say hi," Helen grumped. The sheriff had grown up just across the street from the café owner.

"He was," Sammy confirmed. "I tried to ask him about the Holland case. Normally, he doesn't seem to mind, but he got all weird about it. The only thing he would tell me is that they found a bolt in the street near the scene of the crime, but he insisted it wasn't important."

"Then maybe it isn't." Kate gestured at her with the spoon from her own dish of ice cream. "No offense, Sammy, but he's been in this field a lot longer than you have."

That seemed perfectly reasonable, but not in light of what else Sammy knew. It was time to talk about it. "Yes, that's true, and I would certainly hope the sheriff knows more about solving crimes than I do. But I've been thinking a lot about this case already, and I think Blake Hendricks is a solid suspect."

"The mechanic? Why's that?" Helen scooped another bit of ice cream onto her spoon.

Sammy was glad nobody was automatically dismissing the idea. "It's mostly just gossip, but I found out that Blake is an alcoholic. I heard it, and then I could smell it myself on his clothes when I went to check on my car. Someone who's under the influence probably isn't driving well or thinking reasonably."

"But there could be any number of drunks out on the roads, much as I hate to think about that," Kate pointed out.

"Yes, but are there any who used to work for Jimmy Holland and who might have a vendetta against him for firing them? I've heard from two completely separate people that Blake used to work at Holland Motors, and they didn't part on good terms."

Helen gave a short laugh. "That makes almost everyone in this town a murderer. I don't think there were many people who exactly got along with that man. And what about the bolt?"

"I've been thinking a lot about that, too. There are all sorts of junky cars sitting around at A-1 Auto, the type of cars that would probably fall apart pretty easily if they hit something. Plus, the sheriff said there wasn't any evidence of paint on Holland's body. And there wouldn't be, if there was no paint to rub off in the first place. Plenty of those cars are nothing but rust. Honestly, I'm surprised nobody has been pointing the finger at Blake so far."

"Hm. Seems like an interesting assessment." Kate ran her spoon around the bottom of her bowl, catching the melted part. "Why didn't you just come out and tell Jones this."

"He seemed so upset with me," Sammy explained. "I don't know why."

Helen laid a hand on Sammy's arm. "He's jealous, dear."

"Jealous? It's not like I'm going to step in and take credit for the case," she replied.

"No, no," Helen laughed. "He's jealous of your outing with Rob."

"The produce stand again?" Seriously, this was ridiculous. "Why would he be jealous of that?"

Her boss winked at her. "I guess you'd just have to ask him."

Sammy finished her ice cream, her mind heavy with thoughts as she went about her work day. Sheriff Jones couldn't possibly be jealous in *that* way, could he?

9

A1 AUTOS

S ammy walked over to A-1 Auto as soon as she got the call from Blake. She was enjoying what little use she got of the Honda, but she was still eager to pick up the Toyota. And, to be honest, she wanted to talk to Blake. The idea of talking to someone who was a murder suspect should've scared her, and in other times it would have. But she was too curious to worry about her own personal safety for the moment.

"Hey, there!" he said when he saw her walking up. Blake wiped his hands on a rag and gestured to her car, sitting next to the building. "She's all fixed and ready to go, good as new. I also had it detailed to make up for the delay."

"You did?"

Blake opened the door to show her the interior. The dashboard had been dusted and polished, all the windows wiped down, and even the tiny slats in the air vents were clean.

"Wow, thank you. You didn't have to do that."

Blake shrugged, still holding his greasy rag. "In a way, I did. I couldn't help it that the warehouse didn't ship the part on time, but this repair took far longer than it ever should have. I don't want you thinking that's the kind of work I normally do. We can head inside and get you all taken care of and on your way."

Sammy knew this was probably her last chance to talk to Blake in person, unless she purposely broke something on her car just to take it back to him. That sounded far more expensive than it was worth. She just needed a few minutes to figure out what Blake might've been doing the night of the murder. "So," she said as she followed him into his office. "Have you been to any baseball games lately?"

"Nah. I don't mind listening on the radio every now and then, but I don't usually get out in big crowds like that." He clicked on his computer, printing up an invoice.

"Yeah, me neither. I'm always looking for something to do around here, though. Any ideas?" She fished around in her purse for her wallet.

"You're asking the wrong guy, honestly. I don't get out much at all."

She looked up at him, meeting his gaze for a long moment and trying to decide if he was telling the truth. "I see."

Blake snatched the invoice off the printer. "Look, I think I know what you're getting at."

"You do?" Sammy held her debit card in the air, a feeble weapon.

He sighed. "Yeah. You probably saw my car out at one of the bars, or several of them. I know how people talk around this town, and I'm sure they think all sorts of things about me. But I'm only out at those places because I'm always trying to get my cousin Charlie out of trouble."

Sammy's face flushed, and not from the heat. She felt about three feet tall. "Oh. I didn't know."

"I'm sure you didn't. I don't really talk about it. But I promised my aunt before she died that I'd do my best to look after Charlie. Unfortunately, he drinks a lot, and he doesn't behave very well when he's had a few in him. All the local bars know to call me when he starts picking fights, and I always show up to drag him home. I even tried giving him a job here to get him on the right track, but it's like he doesn't really *want* to be on the right track."

"Blake, I'm so sorry. That's got to be a lot for you to handle."

He ran his hand through his hair, leaving a dark stain on the blonde strands. "Yeah. And I know how people in this town talk. They all think I'm the drunk. I smell like the bars, and I show up late to my own business because I'm out talking Charlie out of a fight instead of sleeping at home. It's not fair, but it is what it is."

"I see." Sammy paid her invoice, feeling horribly guilty. This information cleared up a lot of things about Blake, but it didn't necessarily exonerate him.

"You're all set." Blake handed her the keys.

Sammy took them, but she hesitated before she walked out. "Hey, I was going to ask you. I found a bolt on the street the other day. It looked like something that might've fallen off a car. Are you missing anything like that?" She watched his face carefully, looking for a twist of rage or a shadow of guilt.

But the mechanic just gestured at the cardboard boxes full of parts along one wall of his office. "It could be from any vehicle, and if it's from one here then I've got plenty to replace it. Got drawers full of them, actually."

"Oh, okay. I won't worry about it, then." Sammy stepped outside, wondering how she was going to figure all this out. There was so little physical evidence, other than the meaningless bolt, and she really wasn't sure how to proceed.

"Hey, Sammy!" Blake jogged out of the building after her. "I almost forgot. I saw that you were driving a new car."

Embarrassment overwhelmed her as she remembered what Blake had said about people who chose to buy a new car instead of fixing up their current ones. "Oh, um, yeah. I'm not totally sure about buying it yet. It's just a temporary thing, you know. Just trying it out," she babbled.

"I get that. I just wanted to offer to look it over for you, make sure everything is mechanically sound. It's a good idea to know exactly what you're getting into when you're buying a vehicle."

"But it's brand new." There were a few miles on the odometer, probably from test drives, but that was it.

"Yes, and I'm sure it's probably fine. But you'd be surprised what you might find on a car, even fresh from the lot." He quoted her a price for an inspection.

It was a reasonable amount, and it could be the deciding factor in whether or not she purchased the new car. "All right. When can I bring it in?"

"Tomorrow would be good."

"I'll see you then."

10

MIXED AUTO-MOTIVES?

"And that's why everyone thinks Blake is an alcoholic, but he's actually just trying to take care of his family," Sammy explained, leaning against the counter in the kitchen.

Helen had come up to her apartment after work to see how things had gone with getting her car back. She sat at the kitchen table with a cold soda, nodding slowly. "That all makes sense. I'd heard some rumors about him, but I'd never really dealt with him directly. It doesn't seem fair that he should get a reputation like that when he's just trying to do the right thing."

"I know. And there were a lot of people who told me not to use him. There's no telling how much these rumors have hurt his business. Yes, there were some issues, but he made it all up to me even though it wasn't his fault." Sammy had always just cleaned her car on her own, and she'd never had a professional detail job. It made her Toyota seem brand-new again and gave her some more misgivings about purchasing the other car.

"If he's as good as you say he is, then I'll be sure to send anyone his way who mentions they need a mechanic. Someone like that, who's trying to do some good in the world, shouldn't be punished for it." Helen took a sip of her soda thoughtfully.

"Unfortunately, while talking with him cleared that up, it doesn't put me any closer to understanding who killed Jimmy Holland." As glad as she was to have her car back, this case was still bugging her.

"Do you still think it was Blake?"

"I'm not sure. I don't want it to be, in a way, but I don't know who else could've done it. I've got to find a way." She tapped her fingernails on the edge of the counter, feeling antsy.

Helen pointed a finger at her, squinting her eyes. "You be careful. You've got a nose for these things, and I can't lie about that. But they have a way of becoming dangerous. If you ask me, you've been too close to getting hurt, too many times."

"Now you sound like Sheriff Jones," Sammy grumbled. She was a grown woman, and she didn't see why everyone thought they could talk to her like a little kid every now and then. But she did appreciate that Helen cared about her. She might be Sammy's boss, but she was also like family.

"Then maybe you should call him," Helen pointed out. "I love Alfie, and I still see him as a little boy riding his bike down the street. I don't want anything to happen to him, either, but he's trained to deal with dangerous people. Call him up and tell him what you know."

Sammy sat down at the table across from Helen. "That would be a great idea, except he can't seem to make up his mind on whether or not he wants me to help with his investigations. Sometimes he's more than happy for my help, and then yesterday it was like he was angry with me for even thinking about it." She didn't particularly like it that Jones had been teasing her for going to the produce stand with Rob Hewitt, of all the ridiculous things.

Helen smiled. "You need to follow your heart, dear, but you also need to try to understand Alfred's. He's a good man, and he wants justice above all else. He also has an ego to protect, just like anybody else does. Give him time, but do what you need to do. As long as you can show up for work the next day in one piece that, is." She patted Sammy's hand. "I wouldn't want to lose my best baker, not at any cost."

Helen went home and left Sammy to her thoughts. She needed someone to speak up, to give her some vital clue, or for a piece of evidence to just fall right in front of her face. How did the real detectives do it? How did they sort out all the everyday stuff all around them and figure out what was relevant?

She didn't know, and she knew Sheriff Jones wasn't about to tell her. She contented herself with knowing she would have to visit the dealership at least one more time. If she couldn't figure anything out about Jimmy's life from the staff, she'd have to try elsewhere.

In the meantime, Sammy sat down with a mystery novel Viola had recommended to her and tried to keep her mind off the case.

The next day, Sammy drove the Honda over to A-1 Automotive for her appointment. She was no longer nervous about being around Blake, but she was a little nervous about the car. The dealership had seemed particularly eager to sell it, both when the owner had talked to her and when Eric was working with her. Granted, they probably would've been happy to sell her anything on four wheels, but it made her wonder if there was something wrong with it that she couldn't see.

"It's pretty," Blake said when she pulled up in front of the garage door, standing back to admire the bright red paint. "Let's see what's under the hood. This won't take long, and you can wait in the office if you'd like."

"Sure, that works." Sammy headed inside, realizing what an opportunity she had. She took the same chair she'd sat in before across from his desk, taking a few moments to look around. The window air conditioner unit was oversized for the room, and it hummed quietly to itself as it kept the place blessedly cool. She didn't notice any security cameras. In big auto shops, there was usually a big window that looked into the garage area. Here, there was only a solid concrete wall, and Blake's loud rock music thumped through it. This was her chance to look in his computer or through his desk drawers. This was the time for her to be a real sleuth and find evidence that Blake had killed Jimmy.

But she couldn't bring herself to do it. She couldn't even get up out of her seat, flooded with shame every time she pondered invading Blake's privacy like that. He seemed like a genuinely good guy. Maybe she just didn't want to believe that he could kill another man, or maybe she was just starting to lose her talent for solving crimes. She didn't know for sure, but she kept envisioning Blake opening the office door and finding her digging through all his documents. It just wasn't going to happen.

By the time he finally did open the door, she was so deep in her thoughts that she jumped.

"Sorry," he laughed. "I didn't mean to scare you."

"Are you done?"

"Yeah, pretty much. Everything looks great. I did check the records for this type of vehicle online last night, just to see if there were any known issues you might need to look out for. Some cars are notorious for burning oil or having numerous recalls, but I didn't see anything that should be a problem." He held open the office door for her as he walked her out to the garage area. "I did see one thing that I found kind of funny, though."

"What's that?" Sammy stepped into the work area, seeing that her car was still on the lift.

Blake led her around the front of the vehicle and pointed up, just underneath the front bumper. "You said you found a bolt the other day, and it turns out *you're* missing a bolt. I can replace it, though. No problem."

"Me? But I didn't..." Sammy paused. She was about to say that she didn't run over Jimmy Holland, because of course she would remember if she had. But Blake wasn't accusing her of any such thing, because he had no idea why the bolt was so important. Nobody did, other than her. She cleared her throat. "Okay. Um, that's good to know. What would cause something like that to happen?"

Blake lifted a shoulder. "They can just vibrate loose over time if they're not tightened down at the factory. When you think about it, even a brand-new car rides around on the back of a semi truck halfway across the country until it gets to the dealership. There are plenty of opportunities for these things to happen. But I can replace it, no problem."

"No!" She cleared her throat again. "Sorry, no. Holland Motors owns the car, and they should have to fix it."

He scowled slightly at the name of the dealership. "It's theirs for the moment, sure, but if you're going to buy the vehicle then it ought to be replaced. And bolts aren't very expensive. I won't charge you anything."

But Sammy was insistent. "No, it's the principle of the thing. I'll talk to them about it."

"Okay, if you insist." Blake lowered the car from the lift and pulled it out of the garage before meeting Sammy in his office to take care of the payment.

Her entire body was shaking, but she hoped it wasn't visible. Something as small as a missing bolt wouldn't be the kind of thing to set someone off like that, not under normal circumstances. But this was most definitely not a normal circumstance. She paid the invoice, knowing for sure now what her decision would be about the car.

"Are you all right?" Blake asked as he handed her a receipt. "You look a little pale. If the heat is getting to you, then you're more than welcome to stay in here for a while. I wouldn't want you passing out on this hard concrete."

But Sammy most definitely was not all right. Her body was rebelling against her. She tried to tell Blake she was all right, but she couldn't. She just pressed her hand to her forehead and wished the feeling would pass.

"Whoa, hey." He jumped out of his chair and retrieved a bottle of water from the mini fridge. He opened it and handed it to her. "Do you need me to call someone?"

"No, that's all right." She took a slow drink of water, and then another, reminding herself that at least she wasn't sitting there with the killer. "I think I'll be all right."

"If you're sure." Blake's narrow face was doubtful. "The weather can really get to people, you know."

"Yes, but this is helping." She took another drink of water, focusing on the coolness of the liquid as it slid down her throat. "Can I ask you something?"

"Sure."

"Why did you leave Holland Motors?" She pressed the side of the bottle against her forehead. She was starting to feel better.

"Oh." He shuffled some papers on his desk. "It was kind of a bad situation. I hate to say anything about it now, and speak ill of the dead, but I guess it can't hurt anything. I worked for Jimmy for a long time, but then he stopped paying me. I thought it was something personal, because he was always kind of a snob and never thought a plain mechanic was on the same level as he was."

Sammy nodded. She could believe that of the man, even though she'd hardly known him.

"Then I found out he wasn't paying any of his other employees, either. It really bothered me, especially because I know some of those people are trying to raise young families. I confronted him about it, and he fired me. I was fine with that, because I was going to quit anyway."

"I see." Sammy closed her eyes, thinking of the receptionist and how she couldn't afford her daughter's birthday breakfast. How awful! Her paychecks were probably behind, and it wasn't as though there were many other places in this town to get a new job. "I don't blame you for leaving."

"I can't say that it's always been perfect. Owning your own business isn't all it's cracked up to be. I'm usually the only one working here. I've already told you I can't rely on Charlie, so it's open to close, every day. I don't have a chance to be sick or take a day off, and if I do, then I just don't make any money. I'm sorry. You don't want me to go blathering on about this stuff." Blake fetched a bottle of water for himself.

"It's all right, and I'm the one who asked. I'm feeling much better now. I think I'll go. Thanks for everything." She took her keys and headed outside, the door closing behind her. But one look at that little red car and she knew she couldn't get back in the driver's seat. She took out her phone and made a call.

"Jones here."

"It's Sammy. I know you didn't want me to look into it, but I'll apologize later. I've found the car with the missing bolt." She pressed the phone close to her ear, the urgency of it all making her feel tense.

There was a long pause on the other end of the line. "You're kidding me, right?"

"I'm not. Not at all. It's a car that was on the Holland Motors lot, and I've got it right here with me over at A-1 Auto." She shuddered to think that she'd been driving the vehicle around for the last couple of days. She'd been about to purchase a murder weapon.

"I see." There was another moment of silence, quiet enough that Sammy thought he'd hung up for a moment. "You do realize that lots of cars could be missing a bolt like that, right? I mean, there's no guarantee this is the right one."

"I know. I get it. But I've even figured out a motive. You don't have to believe me if you don't want to, but I really think this is it." She glanced at the office door, wondering if Blake was going to come out and check on her. He would find out soon enough what she was up to, but she wasn't going to talk to him about it until Sheriff Jones was on the scene.

She could practically envision the lawman swiping his hand down over his face, looking tired and irritable. "I'll be there as soon as I can, Sammy."

"Thanks." She pressed her lips together, feeling a little silly. "And, could you give me a ride back to my place when we're done? Even if you decide this isn't the right car, I really can't drive it anymore."

"Sure. I can do that."

Sammy hung up.

11

UNCOVERED

The dinner hour was slowing down, and Sammy was able to use her time to work on her latest commission. She'd spent a lot of time practicing on cakes, and now she had been asked to create one for a baby shower. She took her time, slowly turning it this way and that on the turn table as she examined each side. The pink, three-tiered monstrosity was covered in a layer of fondant which she'd carefully marked with a scraper to make it look quilted. Tiny edible pearls were nestled into each corner of the quilting. She used one of her new frosting tips to create a frothy ring around the bottom of each layer.

"That's impressive," Kate said as she brought in a load of dirty plates. "I don't think anyone will want to actually eat it. It's too pretty."

Sammy beamed. "I'm not even done yet. I've still got to make a big fondant bow to set on the top, with the ribbons cascading down the sides." She thought the cake looked nice enough at it was, and the bow might be a bit much, but that was what the customer wanted.

"I'm sure there will be other mothers at this baby shower, so get ready to start doing a whole flood of birthday and baby shower cakes. They're going to go crazy over it. Oh, and you could do gender reveal cakes, too, where the outside of it is plain but the inside is pink or blue!" She clapped her hands with excitement.

Sammy would have done the same if her hands hadn't been full of frosting. "It's an exciting idea! I just love doing this stuff. I feel like I'm really creating something."

Helen stepped into the kitchen, throwing a towel over her shoulder. "Sammy, there's someone here to see you."

She gave Helen a quizzical look but set down her piping bag and pushed through the door to the dining room. Sheriff Jones was sitting at the end of the counter, and he looked up at her. Since nobody else was paying the least bit of attention to her, Sammy had to assume Helen was referring to him.

"I don't suppose you have one last slice of that strawberry rhubarb pie, do you?" he asked quietly.

Sammy pursed her lips, wanting to throw out some remark about not going to the produce stand with Rob recently. But the sheriff seemed like he was there to play nice, so she would, too. "I do." She dished up a piece and put it in front of him.

He picked up his fork, sinking it into the flaky crust. "I thought you'd want to know that we've got everything wrapped up."

"Yeah?" She straightened a set of salt and pepper shakers. Sheriff Jones had indeed shown up at A-1 Auto, much to Blake's surprise. He'd taken the car down to the impound lot so it could be examined. As promised, he'd then given her a ride back to her place, but it had been an awkward one.

"Yeah. The bolt wasn't much to go on, even knowing that it was missing from the Honda. But it did give us a specific car to look at. When we went to the dealership to talk to them about who would've been driving the car on the night in question, one of the salesmen broke right down and confessed."

Sammy stopped pretending to work and looked at the sheriff. "Which one?"

"Eric."

Her shoulders slumped. "I hate to hear that. He seemed like a pretty nice guy." She knew part of that was just his job, since he wanted to sell her a car and get commission. But that didn't mean it was completely fake.

"Sure, but people get angry when they're not getting paid. You were absolutely right about that one. It turns out Jimmy Holland was making a lot of people mad that way. Eric said he was watching all his coworkers suffer, and then he started falling behind on his mortgage. To top it all off, Jimmy would dive in and try to make as many of the sales himself as he could, just so he wouldn't have to pay commission."

"That's pretty bad. What's going to happen to the dealership?" She thought of the receptionist and her daughter, who relied so much on that job.

Jones tipped his head from side to side. "I think some family member will step in and either take over or sell it off. I'm not sure yet."

"Okay. Well, I appreciate you letting me know." She started to move off to let him enjoy his pie in piece.

He stopped her with his hand on her arm. It was warm and strong, and her heart jumped a little when she turned to meet his dark blue eyes.

"Sammy, I owe you an apology. I was crabby with you when you tried to ask me about the case before, and I shouldn't have been."

She pulled in a deep breath. "It's all right. I shouldn't have been sticking my nose where it didn't belong. Again." Sammy thought about what Helen had said, that Alfred had an ego to protect as well as his heart. He was much more than just a uniform, and she needed to remember that.

"Well, that's debatable. What it comes down to is that I should be more grateful for your help. It's just that you're a little too good sometimes, and the higher-ups are starting to question how I'm coming up with these hunches. They think I'm either some super detective, or else I'm in on the jobs."

Her eyes widened. "How could anybody think that?"

"It's just too coincidental, and of course I can't tell them that the pretty girl at the bakery is helping me out." His cheeks colored slightly.

So did hers. "I didn't mean to get you into trouble."

"No, don't think about it like that. I just need to start doing a better job of figuring these things out before you do." He smiled and went back to his pie. "What did you decide to do about your car?"

"I'm just keeping my Toyota. I got pretty caught up on the idea of getting a new vehicle, but now that my own car is working fine again, there's not much reason to. Why take on a payment if I don't have to? Besides, I think I would miss the cargo space. It would be a lot harder to get cakes and pies into the back of a little coupe." She thought about the towering pink cake in the back of the restaurant and how the fondant would look splattered all over the tiny backseat of the Honda. No, it was much better off in her SUV.

"Well, if you change your mind, I'm more than happy to help you get to a dealership in another town. I mean, I doubt you're interested in going back to Holland, even if they open up again."

"You're right about that! I'll keep it in mind. I've heard you do get a better deal in the big cities, but I think there's plenty going on right where I'm at." She looked around at the dining room, seeing the odd array of people she'd grown so accustomed to seeing on a regular basis. There was no need to go to a big city to find excitement that was for sure.

Sheriff Jones pointed with his fork at the pie plate, which was nearly empty. "This is amazing, by the way. I promise I won't ever make fun of you for going to a produce stand again if this is what you're making out of it."

Sammy laughed. He could be just impossible sometimes. "You know what they say. Promises are like pie crusts, easily made and easily broken. I'll get you another slice, on the house."

THANK YOU FOR CHOOSING A PUREREAD BOOK!

We hope you enjoyed the story, and as a way to thank you for choosing PureRead we'd like to send you this free Special Edition Cozy, and other fun reader rewards...

Click Here to download your free Cozy Mystery
PureRead.com/cozy

Thanks again for reading.

See you soon!

If you loved this story why not continue straight away
with other books in the series?

Dying For Cupcakes

Rolling Out a Mystery

Christmas Puds and Killers

Cookies and Condolences

Wedding Cake and a Body by the Lake

A Spoonful of Suspicion

Pie Crumbs & Hit and Run

Blue Ribbon Revenge

Raisin to be Thankful

Auld Lang Crime

Stirring Up Trouble

Haunts & Ham Sandwiches

A Final Slice of Crime

OR READ THE COMPLETE BOXSET!

Start Reading On Amazon Now

OUR GIFT TO YOU

AS A WAY TO SAY THANK YOU WE WOULD
LOVE TO SEND YOU THIS SPECIAL EDITION
COZY MYSTERY FREE OF CHARGE.

Our Reader List is 100% FREE

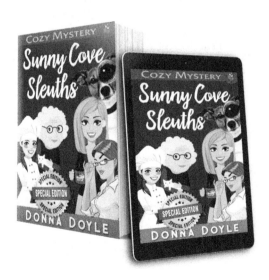

Click Here to download your free Cozy Mystery
PureRead.com/cozy

At PureRead we publish books you can trust. Great tales without smut or swearing, but with all of the mystery and romance you expect from a great story.

Be the first to know when we release new books, take part in our fun competitions, and get surprise free books in your inbox by signing up to our Reader list.

As a thank you you'll receive this exclusive Special Edition Cozy available only to our subscribers...

Click Here to download your free Cozy Mystery
PureRead.com/cozy

Thanks again for reading.
See you soon!

Made in the USA
Monee, IL
19 June 2024

60214687R10075